total immediate collective
imminent   terrestrial
s a l v a t i o n

Sue

to Dorothy, John + Derek
Christoph   2019

Much Love,

Tim Eb

×

[NATIONAL THEATRE OF SCOTLAND]

World Premiere

A National Theatre of Scotland production in association with the Royal Court Theatre, Teatro do Bairro Alto, Lisbon and Attenborough Centre for the Creative Arts (ACCA). Co-commissioned with Royal Court Theatre.

Total Immediate Collective
Imminent Terrestrial Salvation

Written by Tim Crouch
Directed by Karl James & Andy Smith
Illustrated and Designed by Rachana Jadhav

Performers

Shyvonne Ahmmad
Tim Crouch
Susan Vidler

Creative Team

Tim Crouch	Writer
Andy Smith	Co-Director
Karl James	Co-Director
Rachana Jadhav	Book Illustrator & Set Designer
Karen Bryce	Lighting Designer
Pippa Murphy	Sound Designer
Adura Onashile	Artistic Associate
Laura Donnelly, CDG	Casting Director
Yvonne Strain	BSL Performance Interpreter

Production Team

Siobhán Barbour	Production Manager
Emma Skaer	Stage Manager
Hana Allan	Technical Manager
Neil Hobbs	Sound Supervisor

Part of the British Council Edinburgh Showcase 2019

<u>Tour dates</u>

Edinburgh International Festival
7–25 August 2019

Royal Court Theatre, London
3–21 September 2019

Dublin Theatre Festival
2–6 October 2019

Attenborough Centre for the Creative Arts, Brighton
6–9 November 2019

Teatro do Bairro Alto, Lisbon
13–16 November 2019

BIOGRAPHIES

SHYVONNE AHMMAD – Performer
Shyvonne is currently in her second year of training as an actor at the Royal Conservatoire of Scotland. She is the recipient of the Conservatoire's Arnold Fleming Scholarship and is also supported by the Dewar Arts Award. She made her professional debut earlier this year with the National Theatre of Scotland in Cora Bissett's *Interference*.

KAREN BRYCE – Lighting Designer
Karen trained at the Royal Scottish Academy of Music and Drama and she was Technical Stage Manager at Tron Theatre, Glasgow.

Her lighting design credits include *Multiplex, Staircase, Lost, Happy Days, Shall Rodger Casement Hang* (Tron Theatre Company). Previous large-scale projects have included *The Enchanted Forest* in Dunkeld and at Edinburgh Botanic Gardens. She designs lighting for musical icon Horse (Royal Concert Hall, Glasgow City Halls, Fruitmarket and The Barrowlands), and tours. Karen has overseen the pyrotechnics for many large-scale events including Glasgow City of Architecture and Design, Glasgow's Millennium Celebration, Glasgow's George Square Christmas Lights Switch-on and Guy Fawkes. As a Production Manager she worked for UZ Events and National Theatre of Scotland's *Transform* projects in 2009/10. Karen has also designed for the Gaelic Theatre GU LEOR's tour of *Shrapnel* in 2016, Careful by Horse McDonald at the Edinburgh Festival Fringe in 2016 and Careful the Tour in 2017, and Horse's Band Winter Tour in 2107. NTS *How To Act* at the Edinburgh Fringe 2017 and Scottish Tour 2018. Horse gigs 2018/2019. *Pigeon* with Incahootz 2019. Karen also teaches lighting for HNC and HND at West College Scotland.

TIM CROUCH – Writer and Performer
Tim is a playwright and theatre-maker. He was an actor before starting to write and he still performs in much of his work. His plays include *My Arm, ENGLAND (a play for galleries); An Oak Tree, The Author, Adler & Gibb, Beginners,* and (with Andy Smith) *what happens to the hope at the end of the evening.*

Tim also writes for younger audiences. A series of plays inspired by Shakespeare's lesser characters includes *I, Malvolio* and *I, Peaseblossom*. For the RSC Tim has directed *The Taming of the Shrew*, *King Lear* and *I, Cinna (the poet)* – all for young audiences. Directing credits include *Jeramee, Hartleby and Oooglemore* for the Unicorn Theatre, *The Complete Deaths* for Spymonkey and *Peat* for The Ark, Dublin. Tim created and co-wrote *Don't Forget the Driver*, a six-part series for BBC2 which aired in spring 2019.

Awards include a Writer's Guild of Great Britain award – Best Play for Young Audiences 2019, Off-Broadway Obie special citation, a Prix Italia for Best Adapted Drama, an Edinburgh Fringe First, two Herald Angels, two Total Theatre awards, the 2007 Brian Way award for best children's play and he shared the 2010 John Whiting award. Tim is published by Oberon Books.

www.timcrouchtheatre.co.uk

RACHANA JADHAV – Book Illustrator and Set Designer

Rachana is an award-winning theatre designer, illustrator, creative producer and co-artistic Director of Brolly Productions. She trained as an architect and became interested in theatre through her practice in conceptual and spatial design. She completed an MA in Scenography at St Martins College of Art and Design, which allowed her to explore her process and has enjoyed over fifteen years of designing a range of shows including hip-hop basketball musical *Slam Dunk* (Nitro Theatre); one woman show *Curry Tales* (Rasa); Claire Cunningham's *Menage a Trois* (National Theatre of Scotland) and *Random Selfies* (Oval House).

She curated and designed the Alchemy Festival on Tour in Doncaster, her hometown. Her installation works include National Theatre, Southbank, Cast Doncaster and illustration works include *Interactions*, an anthology of short stories and poems with stroke survivors. In 2010 she co-founded Brolly Productions with Dominic Hingorani whose works include one woman show *her* (Half Moon), and new opera *Clocks 1888: the greener* (Hackney Empire). She is currently working on Brolly's second opera *The Powder Monkey* with the National Maritime Museum. Through Brolly, Rachana has been exploring incorporating her original artwork into her theatre practice.

KARL JAMES – Co-Director

Karl has co-directed Tim Crouch's *My Arm, An Oak Tree, ENGLAND, The Author, What Happens To Hope At The End of The Evening* and *Adler & Gibb.*

Most of Karl's time is spent as director of *The Dialogue Project*, with a focus on enabling people to have conversations when the stakes are high. Audio is Karl's passion with his own podcast series 2+2=5 and audio work featured on BBC's radio series Short Cuts, in *A Different Kind of Justice* for BBC Radio 4, at Latitude Festival and in Third Coast's Filmless Festival in Chicago. Karl's book *Say It and Solve It* was published in 2013.

www.thedialogueproject.com

PIPPA MURPHY – Sound Designer

Pippa Murphy is an award-winning composer and sound designer who writes for theatre, dance, screen, choirs and orchestras. She has written music for BBC radio and TV, Celtic Connections, Scottish Opera, SCO, BBCSSO, Edinburgh's Hogmanay and numerous theatre companies including The Royal Lyceum Edinburgh, Perth Horsecross, Dundee Rep, Birmingham Rep, Grid Iron, Stellar Quines, National Theatre Scotland, Traverse Theatre, 7:84.

Her sound design for Karine Polwart's *Wind Resistance* won the CATS Awards for Best Music & Sound 2018 and their album 'Pocket of Wind Resistance' was nominated for BBC Folk Album of the Year 2018.

pippamurphy.com

ADURA ONASHILE – Artistic Associate

Adura Onashile is a Glasgow-based artist whose work is known to Scottish audiences and internationally.

She premiered two sellout shows at the Edinburgh Festival, winning the Scottish Arts Club and Edinburgh Guide Best Scottish Contribution to Drama in 2013 and 2016, a Fringe First award, and has been highly commended for the Amnesty International Freedom of Speech Award.

She has also been nominated for the Alfred Fagon and TOTAL theatre awards and recipient of the Channel 4 playwrights' bursary in 2018 in association with the Traverse Theatre.

She is currently developing new work across theatre, film and television, audience development and international cross-artform collaborations.

ANDY SMITH – Co-Director

Andy Smith is a theatre-maker whose recent works include *SUMMIT* (2018); *COMMONISM* (2017) and *The Preston Bill* (2015).

Andy has collaborated with Tim Crouch since 2004, co-directing (along with Karl James) *An Oak Tree* (2005); *ENGLAND* (2007) and *The Author* (2009). Tim and Andy also co-wrote and performed *what happens to the hope at the end of the evening* together at The Almeida in 2013, and in 2014 Tim, Karl and Andy co- directed Tim's play *Adler & Gibb* at The Royal Court.

Andy has also recently co-directed *Transporter* by Catherine Dyson for Theatr Iolo and *What Good Is Looking Well When You're Rotten On The Inside?* by Emma O'Grady. He lectures in Theatre Practice at The University of Manchester.

SUSAN VIDLER – Performer

Theatre includes *Let The Right One In*; *Knives in Hens*; *Nobody Will Ever Forgive Us* (National Theatre of Scotland); *Trainspotting* (Bush/Citizens/Traverse); *Sabina*; *The Present* (Bush); *The Lover* (Stellar Quines); *A Slow Air* (Tricycle); *Roaring Trade* (Soho Theatre/ Paines Plough); *Petrol Jesus Nightmare*; *Ju Ju Girl* (Traverse).

TV and Film includes *Line of Duty*, *Shetland*, *Dr Who*, *The Adventures of Daniel*, *England Expects*, *The Woman in White*, *Cracker*, *Naked*, *Suspects*, *Hustle*, *Trainspotting*, *Gentlemen and Gangsters*.

The Royal Court Theatre in London is the writers' theatre. It is the leading force in world theatre for energetically cultivating writers – undiscovered, emerging and established.

Through the writers, the Royal Court is at the forefront of creating restless, alert, provocative theatre about now. We open our doors to the unheard voices that, through their writing, change our way of seeing.

Find out more at royalcourttheatre.com

Attenborough Centre for the Creative Arts (ACCA) is an interdisciplinary arts hub in a mid-century modern Grade II listed building, designed by Sir Basil Spence and located on the University of Sussex campus. The public programme includes dance, theatre, live art, music, installation, film, discussion and debate. The programme is guided by the values of Richard Attenborough (former chancellor for the University of Sussex): human rights, social justice, creative education and access to the arts for all.

TBA Teatro do Bairro Alto

Teatro do Bairro Alto is a new city theatre in Lisbon devoted to the development, commissioning and presentation of experimental, emerging and international work, as well as the discourse practices surrounding it. TBA is a meeting place for artists new and established, local and international, working across all performing arts disciplines. TBA's audience is offered tools to be adventurous and wish to come back.

NATIONAL THEATRE OF SCOTLAND

The National Theatre of Scotland is dedicated to playing the great stages, arts centres, village halls, schools and site-specific locations of Scotland, the UK and internationally. As well as creating ground-breaking productions and working with the most talented theatre-makers, the National Theatre of Scotland produces significant community engagement projects, innovates digitally and works constantly to develop new talent.

Central to this is finding pioneering ways to reach current and new audiences and to encourage people's full participation in the Company's work. With no performance building of its own, the Company works with existing and new venues and companies to create and tour theatre of the highest quality. Founded in 2006, the Company, in its short life, has become a globally significant theatrical player, with an extensive repertoire of award-winning work.

Jackie Wylie	Artistic Director and Chief Executive
Seona Reid DBE	Chair

National Theatre of Scotland is core funded by

Scottish Government
Riaghaltas na h-Alba
gov.scot

National Theatre of Scotland, a company limited by guarantee and registered in Scotland (SC234270) is a registered Scottish charity (SC033377).

www.nationaltheatrescotland.com

Part of the British Council Edinburgh Showcase 2019

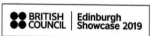

BRITISH COUNCIL | Edinburgh Showcase 2019

First published in 2019 by Oberon Books Ltd
521 Caledonian Road, London N7 9RH
Tel: +44 (0) 20 7607 3637 / Fax: +44 (0) 20 7607 3629
e-mail: info@oberonbooks.com
www.oberonbooks.com

A catalogue record for this book is available from the British Library.

PB ISBN: 9781786828149
E ISBN: 9781786828156

Printed and bound by CPI Group (UK) Ltd, Croydon, CR0 4YY.
eBook conversion by Lapiz Digital Services, India.

Visit www.oberonbooks.com to read more about all our books and to buy them. You will also find features, author interviews and news of any author events, and you can sign up for e-newsletters and be the first to hear about our new releases.

Printed on FSC® accredited paper

10 9 8 7 6 5 4 3 2 1

Dedicated to the memory of Jo Cole and Pauline Knowles.

Parallel Worlds.

There is another world, but it is in this one.
Paul Éluard

A play creates its own world where things can be done differently. Plays are not bound by our natural laws. Time can travel backwards as well as forwards. People become other people; they can die and not die. Teleportation is possible in plays. Multiple states can coexist simultaneously. Things look spontaneous that are in fact intricately predetermined. Plays are self-contained realities with their own codes, their own belief systems and ethical structures – parallel worlds that live alongside our own. This multidimensionality is achieved very simply – not by any complex molecular re-structuring, not by fiendish staging, but through the presence of a story, a form and an observer. Without an observer, the natural laws remain in place, the time travel stays hypothetical, a rehearsal.

The observer is both the creator and the destroyer of these worlds. It's the observer's acceptance that allows the created world to thrive and expand and find its link to the real world. It's the observer who gives licence to the fictions of the created world. Like Lewis Carroll's Queen of Hearts, an audience can 'believe as many as six impossible things before breakfast'.

Our disposition to believe in the parallel worlds of stories is exploited not only by playwrights but also by other spinners of narrative: our leaders. In the face of the uncertainty of our everyday, how much easier is it for us to commit to the story of a parallel world where values can be rendered unambiguous, where original sin can exist, where a wall must be built, where Brexit means Brexit, where the ghost of your dead father exhorts you to revenge his death.

Playwrights are also leaders – dictators, even – no matter how egalitarian they proclaim to be. For the duration of their play, the audience submits to the fictions of their manifesto. It's easier to be led on a subject that holds no singular, objective position. In religion, politics or art, the story can be manipulated because neither god, democracy nor Hamlet has a definitive shape. In this play, Rachana Jadhav has drawn the definitive shape; she's fixed the parallel world;

she has drawn the landscape, the chain fence, the mountain peaks like two cresting waves. She's drawn the people in that world – even if the actors look nothing like them. She's also drawn the audience – a group agreeing to sit together, to read, to confer credibility to the story of a group who sit together conferring credibility to a story. The audience is also a character in this parallel world. Thanks for reading.

Tim Crouch
August 2019

Note for this edition
There are two printed versions of this play. One is exclusively used by the actors and audience in the performance. The actors read most of their lines from that book. They invite the audience to turn the pages with them. They give the audience time to study the illustrations and read the stage directions. The actors don't always represent the physical actions that are described in the text.

The other printed version of the play — this one, the one that you are holding now — contains information like biographies, production details, and this note. In this version, you can see all the lines and stage directions that don't appear in the performance book but that give you, the reader, an idea of the experience of the play with a live audience.

Thanks

Karen Fishwick, Nkhanise Phiri and Claire Marshall. Dr Robert Stockill. Jackie Wylie and the National Theatre of Scotland. Vicky Featherstone and the Royal Court Theatre. James Hogan, James Illman, Konstantinos Vasdekis and all at Oberon Books. Rob Swain and Birkbeck College. Gill Foster and LSBU. Fernando Rubio and Ceclia Kuska. Francisco Frazao at Teatro do Bairro Alto, Lisbon. Laura McDermott and ACCA, Brighton. All the observers and readers: including Phil Cleaves, Théophile Sclavis, Bonnie Chan, Georgia Brown, Alex Prescot, Miriam Battye, Fizz Waller, Steffi Felton, John Retallack, Stephen Wrentmore. Nel, Owen, Joe and Julia.

A circle of chairs.

Each audience member is given a book of the text as they enter.

The actor who plays ANNA enters the circle.

A welcome to the audience:

Hello.

Thanks for coming. Thanks for being here.

You should all have a book. Does everyone have a book?

This book is part of the play. It's part of the play.

There are pictures in the book that also tell a story.

In a minute, we'll all open this book together and we'll invite you to turn the pages together. We'll all turn the pages together.

At some moments during the play we'll invite some of you to read aloud. Is that okay?

Are we good? Are we ready?

Okay. Let's turn to the first page, the title page.

The book is opened.

total immediate collective
imminent   terrestrial
s a l v a t i o n

THIS WINTER

The present time.

Anna
(mum)

Bonnie (age 3)

Miles
(dad)

Felix
(age 5)

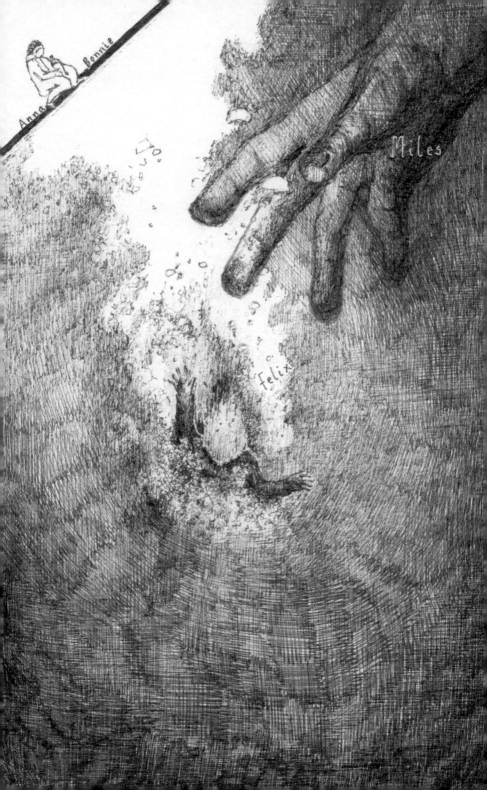

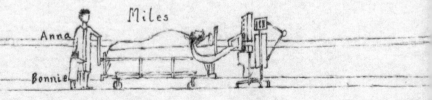

14

THE FUTURE

Two years from the present time
here in this theatre.

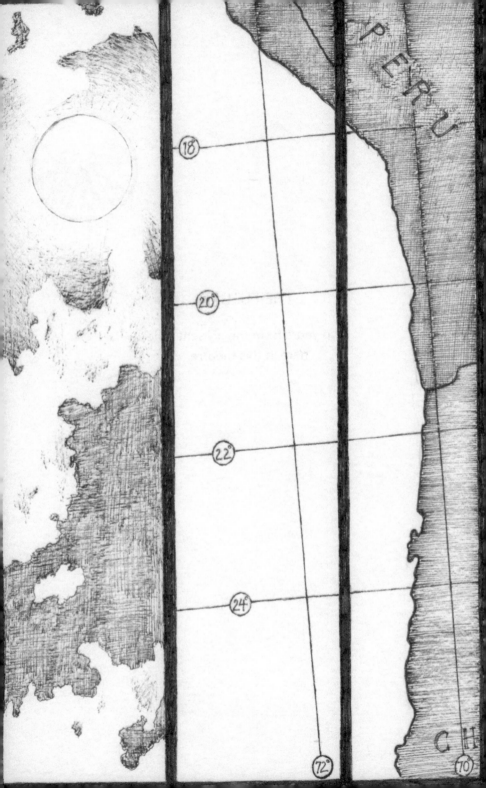

PERU

18

20°

22°

24°

72°

70°

C H

BOLIVIA

ARGENTI

E

68

THE FUTURE

Fifteen years from the present time
here in this theatre.

This is the time in which this play is set.

The action of the play takes place fifteen years in the future from when you're reading this.

Hot sun.

The sounds of the plain.

A young woman asleep on the grass. A book by her side.

Skin sunburned, hair tangled.

An older woman watches the young woman sleeping at a distance.

Heart pounding. Mouth dry.

The older woman has a leather bag over her shoulder.

The young woman wakes.

The smell of earth and flattened grass.

She finds her place in the book.

Some of what she reads may be hard to hear or even inaudible.

The young woman reads:

Eyes.

Blink, eyes, wake.

My place.

Now everything is described.

Near-sight, this last chapter, this. Do not read ahead.

Hello, last book ever. Hello, last words ever. Hello old
buddy. Old body. Last body.

Hello earth, ground, grass, Mum beneath all me.

Feels the heat of the light. Strong heat. Bright. This is the
moment, she remembers. She is empty. Hollowed out.
Virtual. Not much of her left. Not much. A good vessel.

The young woman reads:

A girl kneels on the ground and reads from her book.

Come on, eyes, you disappointments.

This girl is me. Described as me here. Is me. Alone in this spot. In this community. This patch of earth. At the base of this atmosphere. These coordinates so long alluded to.

Can read fast now. Yes can skim, not skip, never skip, clear sight, so hot here, hot, the change is in, is coming in, resolutely in, this girl can feel it, she can. What time it is. What time? This girl feels small but is about to emerge, to change, to slide through out of here, out of her, all of us. Could sing, could sing a praise, could kneel here on the dusty earth and sing a praise to the dark, to the ink dark –

The young woman senses the presence of her father.

The young woman stands up.

She straightens her clothes.

The sun on her skin.

Dad?

The girl reading is eighteen years old.
She has lived in the place where this play is set for thirteen years.
She came to this place when she was five.

A hard place to live.
Hope. Hunger.

Dad?

I thought you were one of the women, I thought – my eyes.

Focus.

Concentrate.

You're rare sir here this patch of this mine you to word beside words besides what words loosened and and spin and and stop this all as written still light light-head Dad you put these these wonders are hold these still these are words mine moving are moving in now honour lines no honours yes did wrong you're seldom your seldom Dad –

Has it begun?

Will the words leave first?

Dad?

Miles?

Stood up too quickly.

What time is it? We're nearly there now, aren't we, sir?
Any minute now, Dad!
You come to fetch me for it?
You come to bring me to the moment?
Dad?
Was having such a dream, Dad. Such a dream.

Eyes slow to adjust right now, can't find their fix.

She studies the page.
She reads with her face close to the book.
She flicks back to the beginning.
She finds her place again.

The young woman reads:

You stay exactly where you are.

I shout, I only have to and they come.

You a tourist? Huh?
An American?
Stumble here by accident, did you?
Get back to your tour bus, lady.
Get back to your hotel room.
Watch it all on TV.

Know what this is?
Know where we are?

Know what time it is?
What's coming?

Not know what's coming?

Are you the dumbest of the dumb?

How'd you get in, anyway? How'd you even get this
close? This land is circumscribed, protected, this area
– That perimeter. Up to the ridge and further. To the
mountains. Can't just walk in. Can't just – Stay back,
serious, or – Stay back.

Are you alone?
Huh?
Do I know you?
Huh?

¿Te conozco?
¿Hablas inglés?
¿Has venido a llevarme?

Have you come to take me?
Kill me? Is that it? You going to kill me?

Fear.

Do you even speak?

I could read ahead but it's not sanctioned.

Fear.

Turn the page, Sol.

Ten minutes before this moment here on stage.

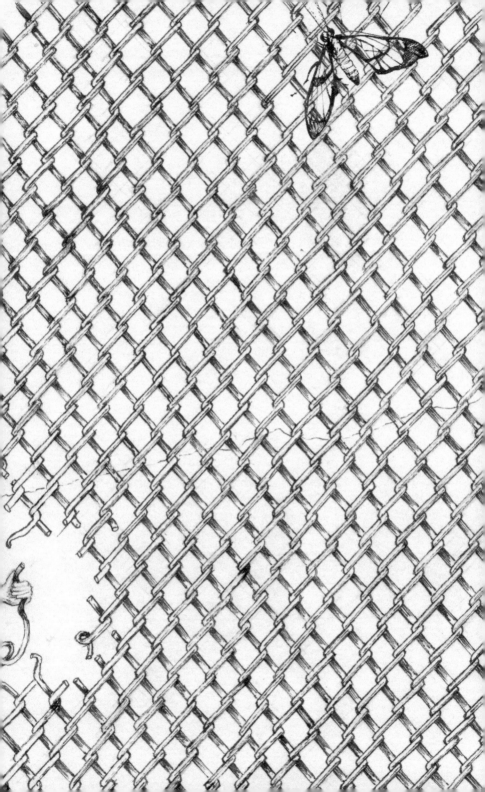

Anna

Young woman SOL.

Older woman ANNA.

ANNA reads from her book.

ANNA   It's just me, look. No one else, look. Look.

SOL   How long were you even there?
ANNA   I didn't want to wake you.
SOL   How long?
ANNA   Not long.
SOL   Sleep is sanctioned.

ANNA   Where's everyone else?

SOL   Prep.

ANNA   Not you?

SOL   I'm ready.

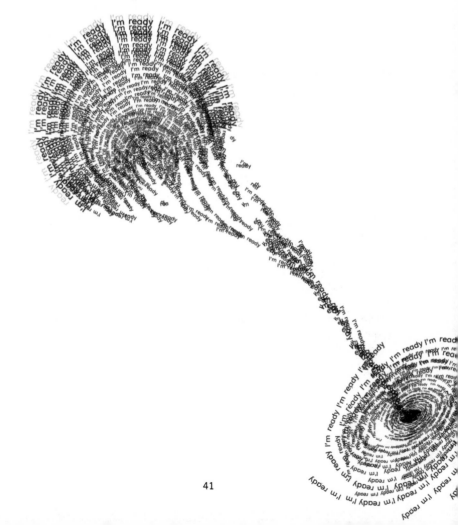

ANNA   I'm guessing you're ready, then.
SOL   Yes, I am.

ANNA   Is that what you're wearing?
SOL   Unless he tells me.
ANNA   You look nice.
SOL   No metal, look.
ANNA   I can see.
SOL   No metal.
        You got metal?
ANNA   Yes. These buttons. This watch.
SOL   You'll fry.

SOL looks to the sky.
Shelters her eyes from the sun.

Nausea.
Needle grass.

SOL   What time is it?
ANNA   Less than an hour?
SOL   Less than!

SOL shakes uncontrollably.

ANNA	Are you alright?
SOL	I have to go. The final meeting.
ANNA	He'll come and get you, won't he, when it's time. He'll call for you.
SOL	–
ANNA	He won't let you miss it.
SOL	Can't miss it.
ANNA	Not this!
SOL	No.
ANNA	Not today of all days.
SOL	No.
ANNA	Sit beside him!
SOL	Yes.
ANNA	You and him.
SOL	Yes!
ANNA	Side by side.
SOL	In the middle.
ANNA	His sunbeam.
SOL	–

SOL wipes sweat from her face.
Nails bitten. Wrists thin.

SOL looks to the edge of the area.

She looks up to the mountain ridge. The tree line. She chews at her lip.

ANNA   Are you nervous?

SOL straightens her dress.
She presses her hands against her legs.

SOL   Are you a critic?
ANNA   No.
SOL   Shit-stirrer?
ANNA   –
SOL   Saboteur?
ANNA   Do I look like a saboteur?
SOL   What then?
ANNA   –

SOL breaks off a blade of grass and lets it drop.

SOL   Where are you from?
ANNA   Europe.
SOL   And me.
ANNA   Yes.
          You're famous, you are, this place, your dad. In the papers,
          you are. On TV. Did they tell you?
SOL   –

ANNA	I flew to see you.
SOL	So?
ANNA	Twelve hours, a long way, a train. A bus. Wanted to come here forever.
SOL	What stopped you?

ANNA steadies herself.
Her throat tightens.

Book heavy as stone in her hand.

SOL	Did you tell him you were coming?
ANNA	He'll know, won't he?
SOL	He wrote all this.
ANNA	So he knows we're talking.
	He'll know I got through the fence, won't he? Cut through, found you sleeping. He'll know what I've been up to all this time and before.
SOL	He's seen the future.
ANNA	He has, hasn't he.
SOL	On each page.
ANNA	Yes.
SOL	He's seen everything.
ANNA	He knows how it ends.
SOL	Everything.
ANNA	Even dreams.

SOL approaches an audience member.

SOL   Could you read?

The audience member reads the following:

> In my dream, I was an ants nest.
> A big hill in the shape of me as I am now.
> With my legs deep beneath the ground.
> It's raining and I'm losing my form with the rain.
> The rain stops and the dream is in colour now.
> This is the day when the ants fly and all of me breaks
> apart and a million bits of me fly into the air.
> And the noise is deafening and I don't know where I exist.
> Just a million winged shapes.

SOL   See?

        (Off book.) They weren't ants. They were termites.

SOL shivers.

SOL brushes hair away from her face.

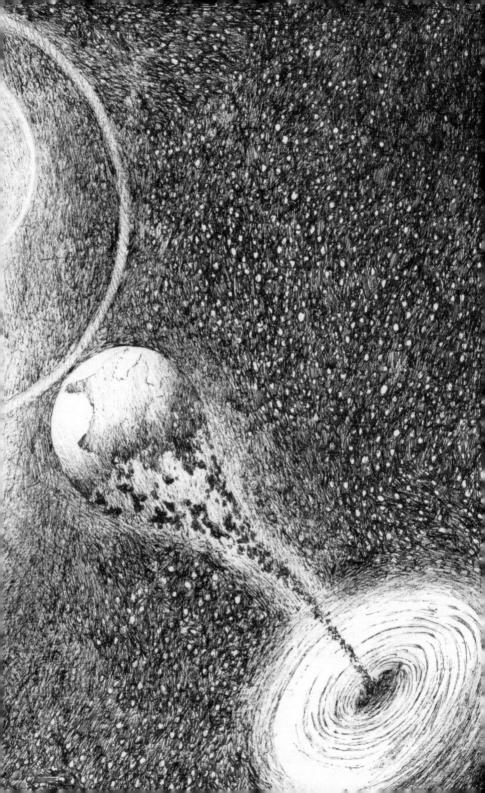

SOL	Having such visions.
	The men, even.
ANNA	Even the men.
SOL	Everyone sleeping more and more.
ANNA	Are you ill?
SOL	Charging.
ANNA	You don't look full.
SOL	Fuller than full.

SOL doubles over.

A large bird circles high above them.

The pain passes.

ANNA	Your period?
SOL	Not anymore.
ANNA	Since when?
SOL	All the women.
ANNA	Is he giving you stuff?
SOL	Supplements.
ANNA	Where does he get those from?
SOL	Why am I even talking to you? Why am I even talking?
	What time is it?
ANNA	Not long now.
SOL	You here to convert me?
ANNA	Are you hungry?
SOL	A missionary?
ANNA	No –
SOL	Going to give me a wafer?

ANNA	No –
SOL	Evangelist, are you?
ANNA	Please.
SOL	Stay back. Stay back!
	You here to save me at the / last minute?
ANNA	Bonnie.
SOL	You think you're going to bundle me into a car? You going to pray for me? It's a bit late for that. Jesus didn't die so we could be reborn, lady, the stars did. The stars.
ANNA	Bonnie.
SOL	You are so dumb, lady. There is such ignorance. This is the time of fulfilment. This is the moment. I'm not afraid of what's coming. I will see paradise today.

Barely the strength to stand.

| ANNA | Here. |

ANNA goes to open her bag.

| SOL | Don't move. |
| ANNA | No harm. Nothing. |

ANNA puts her book down.
She empties the contents of the bag onto the dry grass.
A soft toy, a pair of glasses, some food.

| SOL | Step away. |

SOL puts her book down.

> *(Off book.)* This is not sanctioned.

SOL eats.

A cloud passes across the sun.
ANNA checks the surroundings.
She moves to take SOL's book.
SOL retrieves her book.

SOL   Were you here?

ANNA   How have you been?
SOL   This is where I live.
ANNA   How is that?
SOL   These are his direct words.
ANNA   Yes.
SOL   My words.

ANNA   You want to put it down again?

SOL   We don't know what to say – we might say anything –
stupid things, dumb things, you know. And then this says
– he knows – Before this there could be any infinite any –
And then this. This has been thought through. Each page
literal. You can't select – These words with daily diligence.
We are his patterns, you understand. All of us. Because
he – This is true. This is being said. Now. Each word for a
reason. Each word reveals – contains the principle. Before,
endless random possibilities and then this. No word
without purpose. Nothing you say without reason.

Anna

DARK

MATTER

The glasses.

SOL	Not sanctioned.
ANNA	Since when?
SOL	No lenses. No distortion.
ANNA	He says?
SOL	It says.
	Talk to him.
ANNA	If he wanted to talk to me he'd be here, wouldn't he? He'd have written the conversation.
SOL	He has no time now, does he?
ANNA	No.
SOL	This is everything.
ANNA	Yes.
SOL	He's the father.
ANNA	He's your father.
SOL	Mine, yes.
	Everything is determined.
ANNA	No question?
SOL	This is the day!
ANNA	You're ready!
SOL	You're coming, too, lady! Everyone. But you'll burn with your buttons.

SOL gives the glasses to a member of the audience.

SOL doubles over.

Concentrate.

ANNA   You've eaten too quickly.

SOL   Flesh is first out all static over physical this this spectrum
         fields of force this over time this particle can't can't and
         if can't if p has a definite value your hands these legs this
         skin all values of q equally probable if q has a definite −

The large bird dips lower in the sky.

SOL   The last meeting.

ANNA   Sleep is sanctioned.

SOL stares at ANNA.

The young woman called SOL was once called Bonnie.

SOL lies down on the grass and sleeps.

ANNA approaches an audience member.

Different members of the audience read SOL.

ANNA   How many of you are there now?
SOL   Ninety or so.

ANNA approaches another audience member.

ANNA   No tensions?
SOL   No more than any group.
ANNA   No divisions?
SOL   If people are unhappy they can leave.
ANNA   They're free to go?
SOL   No one's here against their will.

ANNA approaches another audience member.

ANNA   How many have left?
SOL   They also join
        They study us.
        We publish online.
        In journals.
ANNA   I read them.
SOL   They understand our position.

ANNA approaches another audience member.

ANNA	And the community?
SOL	In here?
ANNA	Outside of here. The indigenous people.
SOL	We tried to involve them.
	We held meetings.
	Made applications.
	Sent invitations.
ANNA	What happened?
SOL	We gave up.

ANNA approaches another audience member.

ANNA	You speak Spanish.
SOL	They don't listen.
	They're ignorant.
	Uneducated.
ANNA	You think?
SOL	We talk to the world.
ANNA	Of course.
SOL	People make their way to us. They find us.
ANNA	Like me.
SOL	Sometimes journalists search for abuse here. They sit down among us. They try to discredit us. Expose us. You look around at the group. You look in their faces. You can see in their faces.

ANNA looks towards the low buildings in the distance.

A cap of white cloud spills from the mountain peaks.

ANNA   Are you just saying what you've been told to say?
SOL   No.

ANNA approaches another audience member.

ANNA   You were here first?

SOL   The very first.

ANNA   No other children?

SOL   Are you a reporter?

ANNA   No.

SOL   You should leave.

ANNA approaches another audience member.

ANNA   No other children?

SOL   I'm the youngest.

ANNA   What happened?

SOL   It's not sanctioned.

ANNA   What?

SOL   Children.

ANNA   Since when?

SOL   He says.

ANNA   Why?

SOL   There was a breach.

ANNA   People left?

SOL   Yes.

ANNA   Just once?

SOL   Ten years ago.

THE BREACH

Ten years before
this moment here
on stage.

Bonnie

Miles

64

ANNA approaches another audience member.

ANNA	What do you remember?
SOL	I was eight.
ANNA	Nothing?
SOL	They took the infants.
	My arms were grabbed.
	I resisted.
	They wouldn't dare.
	I'm his daughter.
	I'm the first.
ANNA	Yes.
SOL	He loves me.

ANNA approaches another audience member.

ANNA	Are you happy here?
SOL	Shall I tell you a secret?
ANNA	If you want.
SOL	Someone was killed.
ANNA	Goodness.
SOL	A woman was killed.
ANNA	Was she now.
SOL	Yes. They had to. She would have taken me. Destroyed this.
ANNA	I'm sorry to hear that.
SOL	That's when they paid attention.
ANNA	I imagine.
SOL	That's when they built the perimeter.

ANNA approaches another audience member.

ANNA	Maybe the woman who was killed was trying to help you.
SOL	We don't need help.
ANNA	Were they right to kill her?
SOL	The same would happen now.
ANNA	Maybe she lost her faith.
SOL	There's no faith involved.
ANNA	No?
SOL	This moment was fixed before the continents were formed.

ANNA approaches another audience member.

ANNA	And your mother?
SOL	What time is it?
ANNA	Your mother?
SOL	The woman **was** my mother.
ANNA	Your mother was killed?
SOL	She tried to take me.
ANNA	In the breach?
SOL	She tried to wreck this.
ANNA	Did she.
SOL	She's buried beneath this grass.
ANNA	She is.
SOL	Yes.

ANNA	It's nearly time, isn't it?

SOL gets up.

SOL reads.

SOL   Keep your distance. Keep your distance.
                   I don't need this, today of all days.

ANNA   What will happen today?
SOL   Why am I even talking to you?
ANNA   Because it's written down.

                   Because I'm interested to know.

SOL   We transfer.
ANNA   What will actually happen?
SOL   Isn't that enough?
ANNA   It's what you believe.
SOL   It's what I know.
ANNA   It's what he's told you.
SOL   It's what he saw. You can't break me. He's been there
                   and he came back. He died and he came back.

ANNA   Your dad was in an accident.

SOL   He died.

ANNA   No. Doctors saved him.

SOL   He came back.

ANNA   Doctors using science kept him alive.

SOL   You said it.

ANNA   What?

SOL   Science.

ANNA   –

SOL   You are so dumb, lady. He saw everything. This place,
            the mountains, the shadow coming.

ANNA   His heart stopped but he didn't die.

SOL   This is not superstition.

ANNA   I'm not saying that.

SOL presses the heels of her palms into her eyes.

A gust of wind.

ANNA takes a step towards SOL.

SOL   I know it will start to get dark. It will get colder. The
               sound will change. The birds will stop singing. We will
               sit here. My dad and me. The eclipse will arrive at 1000
               miles an hour. It will intensify until it's total. At the apex –
               For an observer, we would still be here. For the observer,
               time would stretch and we would still be here. A second
               would halve. And then halve again. And then again and
               again and again and again, with us perceived to be
               sitting here. Time would never pass, but split infinitely.
               For an observer, we would always be here forever.

ANNA   But there will be no observers.
SOL   No.
ANNA   And it will be dark.
SOL   Yes.

ANNA   And what happens to you? Inside you?

SOL   We enter paradise.

ANNA   How do you know?

SOL   The Einstein tensor plus the cosmological constant times the metric tensor is 8 pi times the gravitational constant over the speed of light to the fourth power times the stress energy tensor.

ANNA   And what exactly will that look like?

SOL   What time is it?

ANNA   You said you had to go.

SOL   Yes.

ANNA   The last meeting, you said.

SOL   I can't go until this tells me.

They negotiate the turning of the page.

ANNA	Will you see your mother again?
SOL	And my brother.
ANNA	Your brother.
SOL	Felix.

ANNA	Do you remember him?
SOL	I was three.
ANNA	No memory?
SOL	He's the guide.
ANNA	What does that mean?
SOL	He's there already.
ANNA	Where?

Where, Sol?

You mean he wasn't saved – in the accident, he drowned. Your father tried to save him but he failed.

SOL	It's not paradise like you think. It's not choirs of angels. It's not aliens behind the tail of a comet.
ANNA	What then? What exactly is it?
SOL	It's us in altered form.

An audience member shifts in their seat.

SOL	When the shadow arrives, we're at the point where it pulls us in and then we're there. Like that. And nothing gets out.
ANNA	This is a black hole you're talking about.
SOL	It's physics.
ANNA	How do you know?
SOL	Convergence.
ANNA	Here?
SOL	If not here, then somewhere just like here.
ANNA	But also here.
SOL	Both, yes.

ANNA	You believe that?
SOL	Belief is the end of intelligence.
ANNA	What are we, then?
SOL	Infinite possibility.

He's waiting for me.

ANNA	Bonnie.
SOL	My name is Sol.

ANNA	Did you wear glasses once?
SOL	Why have you come here?

Anna 1 week later

THE BREACH
10 years ago

Anna 5 hours later

Anna 2 days later

Anna 1 month later

Anna 2 months later

Anna 3 years later

Anna 4 years later

Anna 5 years later

Anna 6 years later

Anna 8 years later

Anna 9 years later

Anna 10 years later

Anna 2 days ago

Anna yesterday

ANNA takes the glasses from the audience member and offers them to SOL.

ANNA   *(Off book.)* And then we smash them. We –
SOL   *(Off book.)* I need to get back.
ANNA   *(Off book.)* Just try.

SOL puts on the glasses. She looks at ANNA. She looks at the book.

     (Off book.) Read ahead.

SOL skips forward to the end of the book.

     (Off book.) I'd love to hold you if you'd let me.

SOL finds her place..

SOL   And you wait till now to come?
ANNA   Bonnie.
SOL   You wait till now?
ANNA   I tried.
SOL   Today.
ANNA   Yes.
SOL   The last hour.
ANNA   I'm sorry.
SOL   The last minutes.
ANNA   I had to.
SOL   Second thoughts?

ANNA	I came to get you
SOL	Don't want to be got.
ANNA	After, I mean.
SOL	Hedging your bets?
ANNA	No.
SOL	You don't exist here. You died. You got written out. No one mentions you anymore. Not in the readings, not in the –
ANNA	Sol.
SOL	We know what kind of a person you are.
ANNA	I should have come years ago.
SOL	Why didn't you?
ANNA	I tried.
SOL	Not very hard.
ANNA	Listen.
SOL	Not very fucking hard.
ANNA	Love.

SOL	What am I standing on?
ANNA	Love.
SOL	What am I standing on?

The words on this page spiral in, distort and become unreadable.

ANNA He wrote to me, your dad. Miles. He said you didn't want anything to do with me. He wrote. He wrote. I sent stuff, but I assumed you didn't want it or – You were eight. I was worn to a shred. I didn't fight enough. I didn't fight. Maybe thirty of us left. The women. Mostly women. The men stayed. They tried to restrain us. No one was killed, love. No one. It was sudden. A sudden loss of pressure. One minute you're with all this – you want to believe it – you don't fully understand but you're with it and then – With the children there. This day. This day. This focus on him, always. What he said he'd seen. I began to – he made us feel stupid – like he had special knowledge. He didn't know. Nobody knows. He couldn't back down, couldn't admit – with your brother, Felix, the tragedy of it. The whole tragedy. I told him not to. The ice. We watched it from the lakeside – you and me. How do you deal with that? Not like this. You don't do this. Not all this. To say I was dead, Bonnie, to say that. To lie to you about me. He should have died under the ice, my husband. He should have died then. With Felix. They all should. I'm sorry. So, I left. I left. I'm sorry. Do you remember any of us? Your friends – Tom and Clem – remember Clem – Cath's daughter – little Clem? Fuck's sake. You and Clem here in the long grass – she's at college now, Clem – your friends, Bonnie. Grew up with you. We walked away. Had to. Howling for you. As we walked. Howling. Inconsolable. To the consulate in La Paz. To hospital for check-ups. And then back home to what. I moved around, love. To the islands. The others settled down, but I couldn't, I couldn't. I'd left it all here. Lost – Wasted so much. I fell apart. Fell apart. I spent years trying to get to him. To you. He didn't tell you? He didn't tell you? I sent you letters, messages, love – and he never gave them to you. I worked so hard to make it better. Thinking you didn't want to know. And all the time this date on the calendar. This day. This hour. Nothing will happen today. Nothing. I'm sorry, I'm sorry. You have twenty minutes left. Go on. The last meeting, you said. Go. This is nothing. I'm nothing. This world will end soon enough.

ANNA and SOL approach two audience members.

SOL   *(Off book.)* Could you read me, Sol?

ANNA   *(Off book.)* Could you read Anna?

SOL   *(Off book.)* Start when I say 'Okay'.

All of the following text is read by two audience members.

SOL   What happens now?

ANNA   I walk out.

SOL   And what do I do?

ANNA   Whatever you want.

SOL   I don't know you.

ANNA   Then stay here.

SOL rubs the back of her neck. Thin, fast breath.

The smell of ozone. Metal in the air.

ANNA looks at her watch.

SOL   And when the eclipse comes?

ANNA   You'll sit in the dark for a bit.

SOL   And if it <u>stays</u> dark?

ANNA   Then everything will have changed and he was right.

SOL   And if the light comes back?

ANNA   Then everything will also have changed and he was wrong.

SOL	Where will you go?
ANNA	Home.
SOL	How?
ANNA	The way I came.
	A bus. A train.
	I bought returns.
SOL	And then what?
ANNA	I'd go back to work.
SOL	And me?
ANNA	You'd stay here, I suppose.
SOL	Yes.
ANNA	You'd feel let down, I imagine.
	Is that it, you'd think.
SOL	Please don't.
ANNA	An anti-climax. After everything he's said.
	Hoping for something more.
SOL	Please don't.
ANNA	Or he re-calculates. And you'd all start again.
	Yes.
	He'll re-write, of course he will.
	And off you go again. New hope. New expectation.

The two actors leave the circle.

The two audience members continue reading.

SOL   He told me you were dead.

ANNA   I came back, didn't I?

SOL   Yes.

ANNA   I'm here now.

          In an altered form.

SOL   Yes.

ANNA   So, he was right, wasn't he?

Marbled clouds. Stillness.

ANNA brushes an insect from her leg.

She tilts her head. Shades her eyes from the sun.

SOL   I don't want to leave.

ANNA   I imagine you'd have some questions.

SOL   I can't.

ANNA   We'd talk it through. On the bus.

          We'd stay in a hotel. A meal. Some ice cream.

SOL   I can't go.

ANNA   We'd get you help.

Take your time.

SOL   What time is it?

ANNA   Less than twenty minutes now.

SOL   Less than.

ANNA   The shadow's nearly here.

SOL   He's waiting for me.

ANNA   None of this is true, you know.

           What he's written here.

           None of it.

           Come with me.

SOL   No.

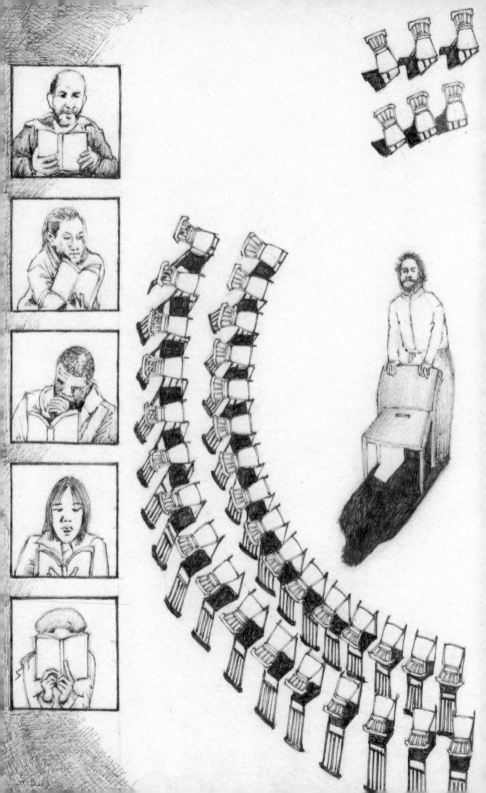

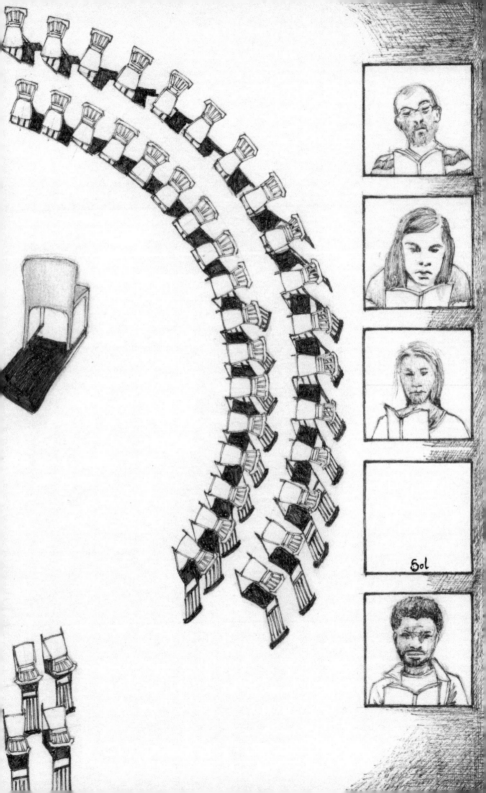

Sol

THE LAST MEETING

Two chairs in the middle of the circle.

No book in MILES' hand.

MILES   Shall we take a moment to breathe?

Look at what we've done. Look at what we've created.

When a small group of us travelled here – arrived here – committed to understanding, convinced of our formulations – I never really imagined we would achieve this much.

Can I hear someone say yes?

An audience member says 'yes'.

Yes.

Thank you!

When I was a little kid in the 1980s there was always talk of a bomb. Anyone here old enough to remember that?

An audience member says 'yes'.

Yes.

I remember there was all sorts of panic among the adults about this bomb. Some people moved as far away as they could from where they thought the bomb would blow. They went to live on islands. Or up mountains.

They were told there'd be a warning. A three-minute warning. Or a five-minute warning. The time it would take for the bomb to get to you. And the talk among the older people was – if you were right between the cross hairs, if you couldn't escape, if even hiding under a table wouldn't help you – the talk was 'what would you do in those three minutes?' And all the virgins would look around desperately at each other. Virgins only need three minutes! And all the religious people would get on their knees. And all the scientists would set up their instruments!

So, we have a fifteen-minute warning. Fifteen light minutes.

And we're not running away. We're not running away because we're running towards. And we're not hiding under tables. Because there's no table big enough in the universe to protect us from what is going to happen in fifteen minutes' time.

Let's set up our instruments.

Can I hear someone say yes?

An audience member says 'yes'.

Yes.

Sol.

First reading,
Who'd like to start?
Who said 'yes'?
You know what page you're on.
Stand up.
Off you go.

An audience member stands and reads.

First Reading
It begins on a lake in winter.
You, Miles, remember nothing.
In hospital, your heart stops.
You see the limitless snail shell of space.
The curve of light.
You see the stars collapse.
You see these exact mountains – like two cresting waves.
You see the sun disappear in daylight on this date.
You see two energy states converge at that precise moment.
You understand everything.

The child who walked out with you on the ice does not come back.

It begins in darkness. It ends in darkness.

Thank you, Miles.

MILES   Thank you. Good reading, yes?

Yes.

Sol.

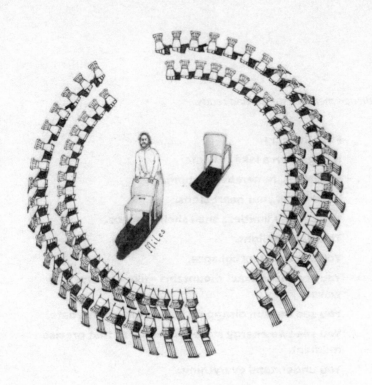

MILES   I sometimes wonder what if science had left me alone!
         If the ice hadn't broken. The same universal outcome,
         but my son would be 21 now. Felix, a young man. Sol
         would have a big brother! And we'd be going through our
         lives, drinking expensive coffees, staring at smartphones,
         rushing around like malfunctioning automatons. Lied to
         by the media. Manipulated and divided by the money-
         grabbers, the politicians. Some of us in temples and
         mosques and churches, no doubt – blithely going along
         with the old fantasies. Far from the peace and certainty
         of where we are now. Look where we are now! There's
         no going back, right? It's too late to walk out now, right?
         Someone?

An audience member says 'yes'.

         Yes.

         You're next!
         In your own time.
         We're here for you.

An audience member stands and reads.

Second Reading
Superstition died with you, Miles.
Against expectations, you revive.
You are in the light at last.
Time and matter one.
You share what you saw.
This date on the calendar.
This moment.
These mountains.
With your daughter, you take to the road.
You hold meetings.
You publish your findings.
The world hears but refuses to listen.
We listen.
You could have left us behind, but you bring us with you.

Darkness is coming again. And, with darkness, new light.
Thank you, Miles.

MILES   Thank you!
           Ten minutes!
           I'm ready. Who's ready?

An audience member says 'me'.

Me.

MILES   Sol.

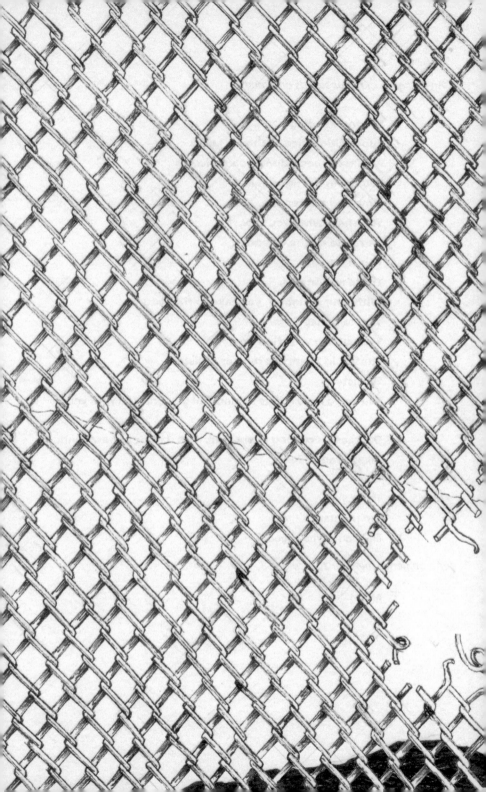

MILES   Throughout millennia, people have proclaimed the coming of the end of the world. At every step, religion has denied the advances of science – freezing us into a single superstitious state. But now science has given us eyes to see. Knowledge has expanded like the universe. Space-time stretched to breaking point. We're going to the place where no world and every world exists. Where the dead died and never died.

Miles, you say, I can't grasp the immensity. Language is inadequate. Maths can hint at it. Equations suggest its shadow. But underneath the ice I saw it.

Sol.

We are somewhere here. When the light goes out we will be everywhere, past and present and future. Everywhere we ever wanted to be. And if it's not us, then it will be us elsewhere. But it will be us.

Can I hear someone say yes?

Yes.

A three-minute warning.

Listen! The animals can sense it now.

So close now.

Last reading.

An audience member stands and reads.

Last Reading
From two given states, a twofold infinity of states may be obtained.

MILES   Yes.

With your son to guide us, we travel to this place.
We settle and prepare.
We study and we build.
We are clear in this community.
We are strong.
We are ready.
We are here for the right reasons.
We trust our calculations.
We sit together and we –

SOL enters with her book.

The reader remains standing.

SOL	I'm sorry. I was asleep.
MILES	I called for you.
SOL	I'm sorry.
MILES	I knew you would be here.
SOL	Yes.
MILES	You know why, don't you?
SOL	Is it coming?
MILES	Of course.

Go on.

The audience member continues reading.

We sit together and we hold our breath.
This is right. We know. Undoubted.

We're ready to pass to the centre.
To cross the boundary of known space-time.
To enter gravitational collapse.
To pass through and into infinite worlds.

Thank you, Miles.

MILES   Thank you.

The shadow is here.

SOL and MILES sit in the two chairs at the centre of the circle.

The results are in.

Thank you for being with me. I wouldn't want anyone else. Thank you for studying so hard, for turning the pages. We got there, didn't we. Can you feel it now? Through the darkness and into the unknown.

With SOL, the audience slowly turn the pages together until the end.

Page by page together.